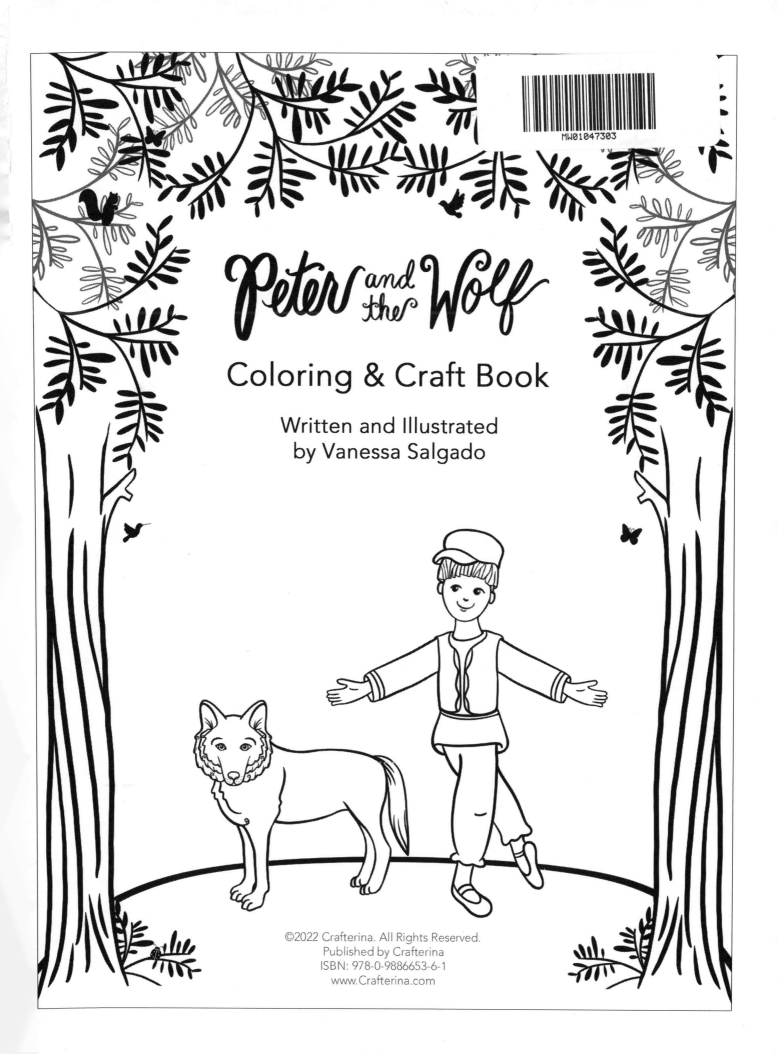

Peter and the Wolf

Coloring & Craft Book

Written and Illustrated
by Vanessa Salgado

Published by Crafterina
ISBN: 978-0-9886653-6-1
www.Crafterina.com

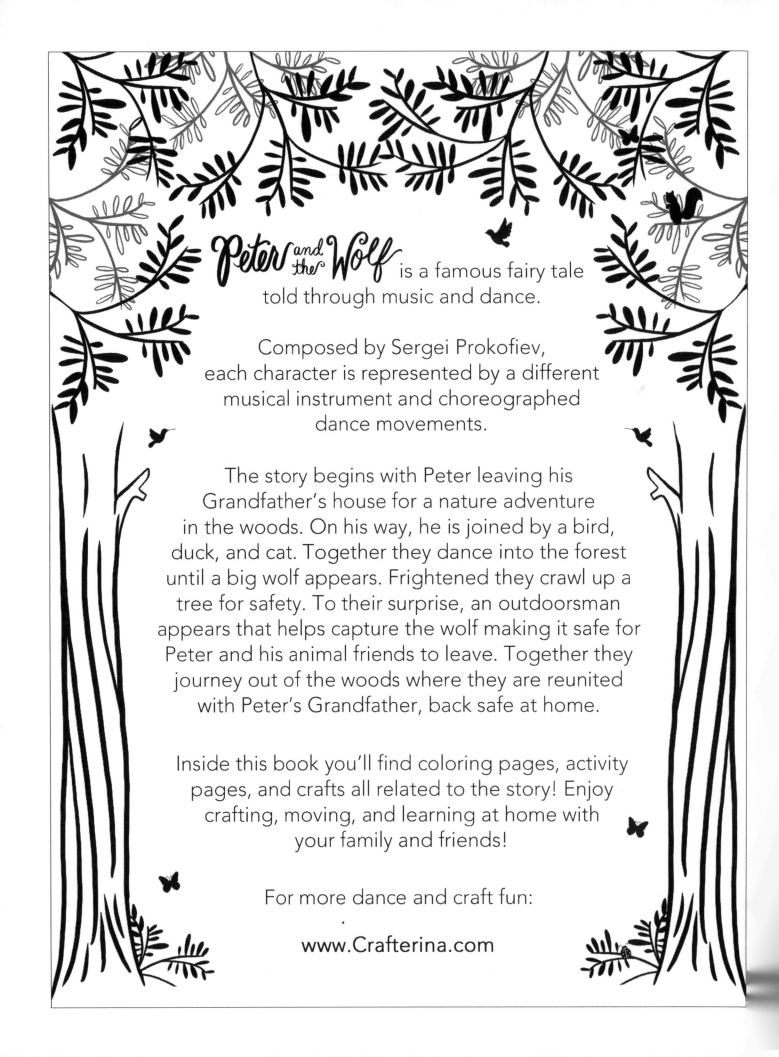

Peter and the Wolf is a famous fairy tale told through music and dance.

Composed by Sergei Prokofiev, each character is represented by a different musical instrument and choreographed dance movements.

The story begins with Peter leaving his Grandfather's house for a nature adventure in the woods. On his way, he is joined by a bird, duck, and cat. Together they dance into the forest until a big wolf appears. Frightened they crawl up a tree for safety. To their surprise, an outdoorsman appears that helps capture the wolf making it safe for Peter and his animal friends to leave. Together they journey out of the woods where they are reunited with Peter's Grandfather, back safe at home.

Inside this book you'll find coloring pages, activity pages, and crafts all related to the story! Enjoy crafting, moving, and learning at home with your family and friends!

For more dance and craft fun:

www.Crafterina.com

Peter

Peter

Grandfather

Bird

Peter and the Wolf

Dancing Bird

Duck

Dancing Duck

Cat

Peter and the Wolf

Dancing Cat

www.Crafterina.com

Peter and the Wolf

Wolf

Peter and the Wolf

Dancing Wolf

Peter *and the* Wolf

Outdoorsman

Peter and the Wolf

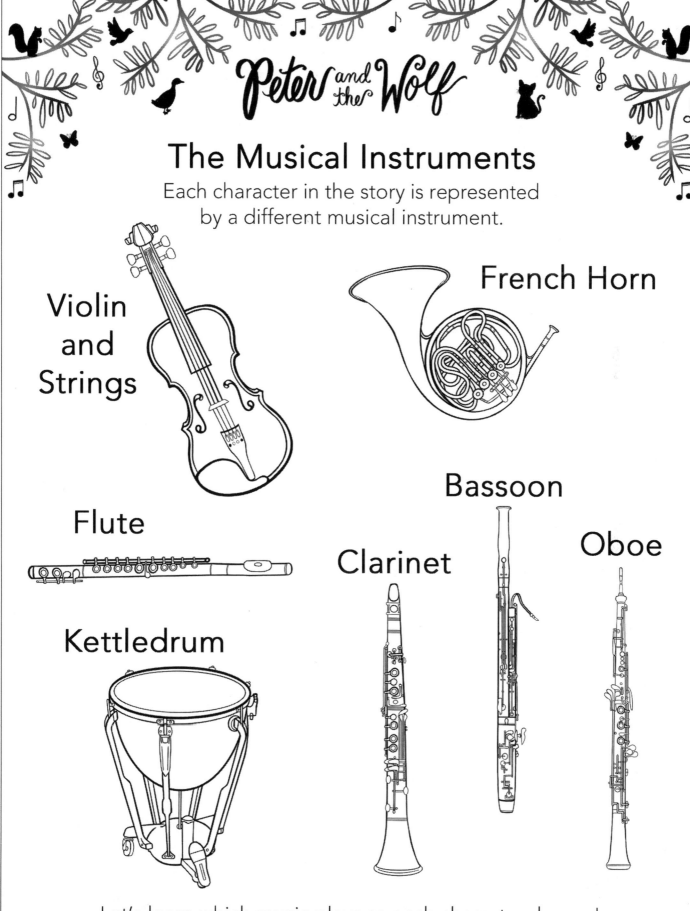

Peter and the Wolf

The Musical Instruments

Each character in the story is represented
by a different musical instrument.

**Violin
and
Strings**

French Horn

Flute

Bassoon

Clarinet

Oboe

Kettledrum

Let's learn which music plays as each character dances!

Grandfather's Music
Listening and Moving Activity

Imagine you are the Grandfather
dancing as the **Bassoon** plays.

Music of the Bird

Listening and Moving Activity

Imagine you are the bird
dancing as the **Flute** plays.

Music of the Duck
Listening and Moving Activity

Imagine you are the duck
dancing as the **Oboe** plays.

www.Crafterina.com

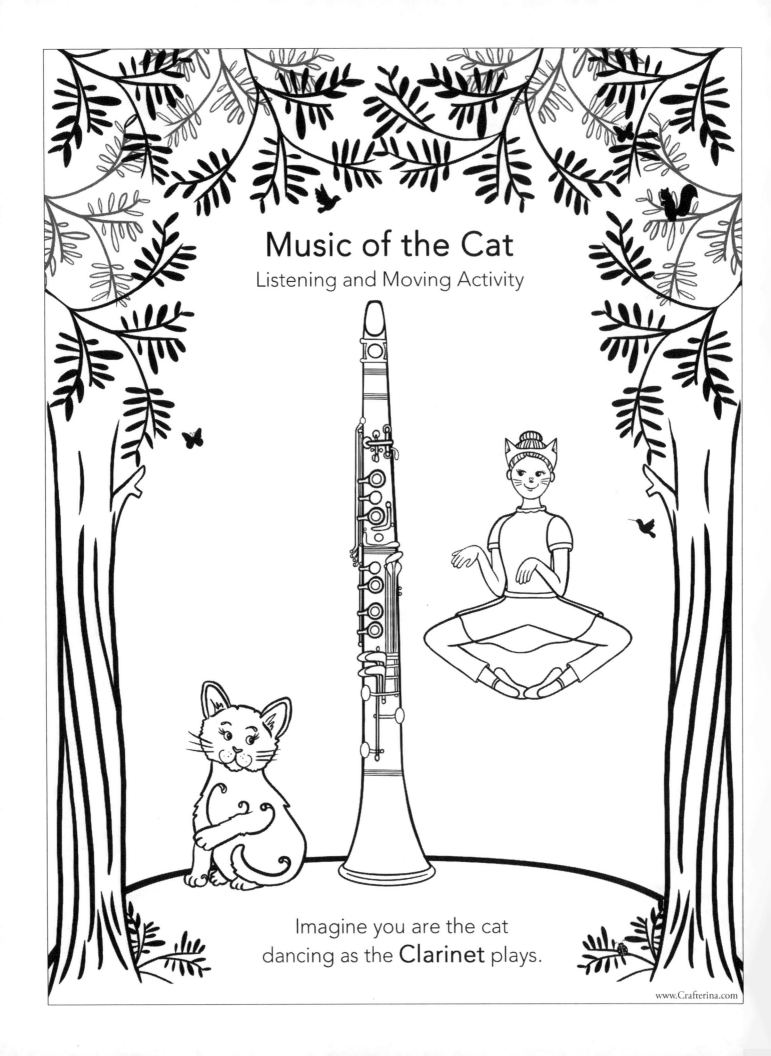

Music of the Cat
Listening and Moving Activity

Imagine you are the cat
dancing as the **Clarinet** plays.

Music of the Wolf
Listening and Moving Activity

Imagine you are the wolf
dancing as the **French Horn** plays.

Outdoorsman Music
Listening and Moving Activity

Imagine you are the Outdoorsman dancing as the **Kettledrum** plays.

www.Crafterina.com

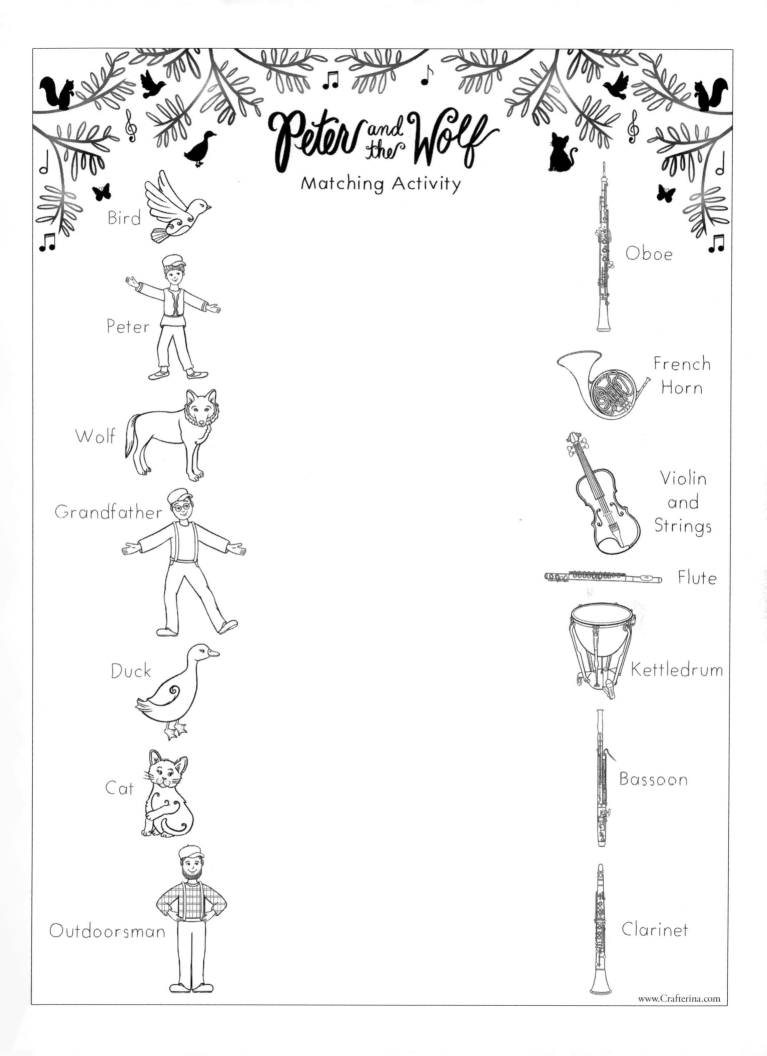

Peter's Favorite Dance Moves

Move like the wind

Spin in the sunshine

Leap over a frog
on a log

Peter and the Wolf

Creative Animal Dances

Fly like a bird

Waddle like a duck

Stretch like a cat

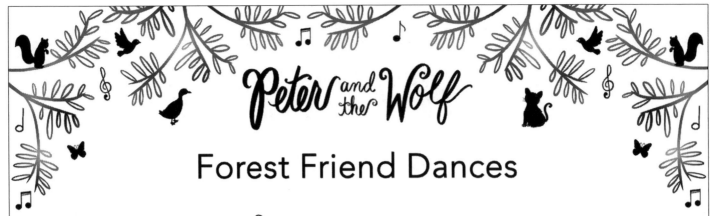

Forest Friend Dances

Fly like a butterfly

Move gracefully like a deer

Tip-toe like a tiny ladybug

Peter and the Wolf

Forest Friend Dances

Leap like a squirrel

Trot like a turkey

Slither like a snake

Let's explore making dance
shapes at different levels.

1. Make a shape that is low to the ground.
2. Make a shape that is in the middle on a medium level.
3. Make a shape that goes high up to the sky.

| Low Level | Medium Level | High Level |

Bonus activity: dance your shape at different levels!

Peter *and* *the* Wolf
Connect the Dots

Peter and the Wolf

Let's create crafts!

Animal Masks

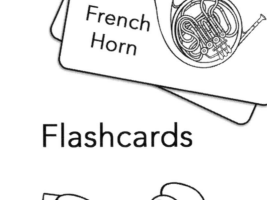

French Horn

Flashcards

Bird Bracelet

Paper Doll

Peter and the Wolf

Dancing Bird Bracelet Craft

Safety Note For Parents: This craft requires parent supervision to create.
There are pieces to cut out and will require your help. Have fun creating together!

Directions:

1. Color and cut out craft

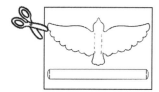

2. Gently bend wings along dotted lines

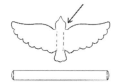

3. Tape together

4. Put bracelet around wrist and move your arm

Peter and the Wolf

Paper Doll Craft

Peter *and the* Wolf

Music and Dance
Flashcards

Wolf

Duck

Peter

Grandfather

Outdoorsman

Bird

Cat

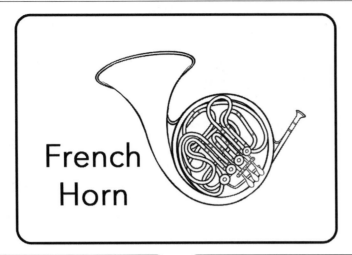

French
Horn

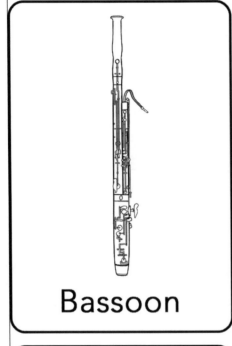

Bassoon

Violin
and
Strings

Oboe

Clarinet

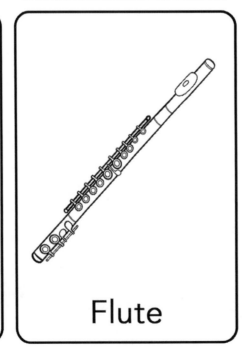

Flute

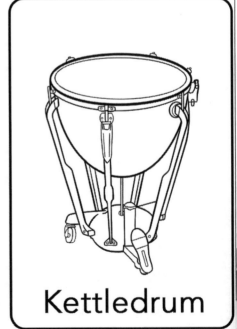

Kettledrum

Peter and the Wolf

Mask Craft Directions

① ✂ - - - Cut out mask pieces

② Fold ear stem ends

③ • Attach ear stems to back of mask with glue or tape
• Bend snout in half and snout tabs down
• Attach tabs to front of mask with glue or tape

You're finished!

Peter and the Wolf

Bird Mask Craft

Peter and the Wolf
Duck Mask Craft

www.Crafterina.com

Peter and the Wolf
Wolf Mask Craft

About the Author

Vanessa Salgado is a Professional Dancer, Educator and Illustrator.

She has taught many little dancers across Manhattan, concentrating primarily at the Joffrey Ballet School, School at STEPS on Broadway, and Alvin Ailey School. She has also worked as an Associate for the Education Department at New York City Center. Vanessa is a graduate of the Alvin Ailey/Fordham University BFA Program at Lincoln Center and holds a certification in Dance Education. Her work has been featured in Dance Teacher Magazine, Dance Spirit, Dance Informa, and METRO US Newspaper, among others.

Her earliest memories involve story time with her dad, creating with her mom after school, and attending weekend ballet class alongside her sister, Donna. Her interests in visual art revealed themselves wholeheartedly in high school as she simultaneously trained for the professional dance world. As she transitioned into her college days and into her professional life, her incessant doodles and crafting have remained a source of wonder for all those around her.

For more information:
www.VanessaSalgado.com

About Crafterina®

Vanessa is also the creator of Crafterina® a series of dance education books and crafts for families. Designed to spark imagination and inspire movement at home, Crafterina® uniquely incorporates reading, creating and dancing in one. Through this interdisciplinary approach, Crafterina® playfully encourages empowerment and teaches youngsters they have the ability to make anything possible.

Inspire a lifelong love for learning in dance with the help of Crafterina®.

For more information, visit our website for books, crafts, and printables:

www.Crafterina.com

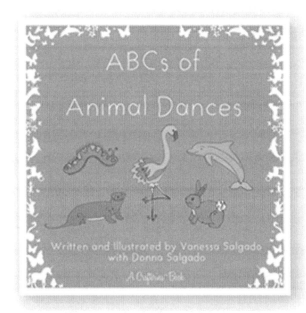

Find more from Crafterina by visiting our website:
www.Crafterina.com

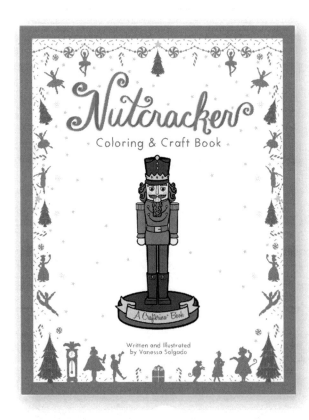

Made in the USA
Monee, IL
07 April 2025

15369723R00028